T0115085

....AND SAT DOWN BESIDE
HER...

...And Sat Down Beside Her

Lynn Thompson

iUniverse, Inc.
Bloomington

...And Sat Down Beside Her

This is a work of fiction. All of the characters, names, incidents, organizations, and dialogue in this novel are either the products of the author's imagination or are used fictitiously.

iUniverse books may be ordered through booksellers or by contacting:

iUniverse
1663 Liberty Drive
Bloomington, IN 47403
www.iuniverse.com
1-800-Authors (1-800-288-4677)

ISBN: 978-1-4620-0540-6 (sc)
ISBN: 978-1-4620-0541-3 (ebk)

Printed in the United States of America

iUniverse rev. date: 3/11/2011

Also by Lynn Thompson

Deep and Dark
…And Along Came A.

Dedications and Acknowledgments

To Mom, who had a black dog of her own
And Kay, who did, too
To Mason, who gets it
To Mark, who expedites it
To Dale, just 'cause
To the rest of the family, thanks for your patience. I think I'm finished now.

CHAPTER ONE

33 percent of dog owners admit that they talk to their dogs on the phone or leave messages on an answering machine while away

The heat snuck into town on humid southern breezes under the Perseid meteors, those bright, hot bits of other worlds. Dew soaked the early morning lawns and sparkled in traps that hunting spiders had set for unsuspecting victims of the buggy sort.

The slow, steady climb of mercury in thermometers outside resulted in adjustments of the thermostats inside and slow, steady whir of ceiling fans.

Cicadas fretted among the wilting leaves, spending their short lives oblivious to the humans who fretted about their garden's decline and their own discomfort. Meteorologists, always popular ratings-grabbers in the broadcasting game, were quoted whenever groups gathered.

"....and, if you will notice, on our map, way out in the Pacific, above good-old Seattle, that swirl of clouds ? Well, that is what our relief looks like. Our own Samantha had her very first job in Seattle, and some of our more devoted viewers may remember the Eyewitness News Team's attempt to be news makers instead of newscasters, last year.........Luckily, we did NOT quit our day jobs.

It all looked so simple: Samantha, raised in foster care in Washington, toddler found covered in the blood of her murdered parents, the time frame.....all of it so perfect............... except for the blood types.............it wasn't....... But, I digress!

"Our breath of fresh air will bring us cooler less humid conditions and a good chance of rain to help out our poor tomatoes..... and give the air-conditioners a rest, finally! We will be able to open our windows and breathe some real air for a change. And, speaking of changes, our beloved Samantha has accepted a position half-way across the nation at one of our affiliates in the Garden State, New Jersey. We will miss her, but we wish her well. She and her faithful companion, Bernard will be the new 'night beat' reporters.

Some of our more faithful viewers will remember when Sam and Bernie got together right here during one of our 'pet of the week' segments. Sam, keep in touch and come back to see us, O.K.?"

Jaych struggled to keep the emotion from spilling out. She and Samantha had developed a bond and a careful friendship.

Off-camera, A.J. the station owner/manager/anchor sniffled. Smitty, big, strong sports-caster, sobbed loudly into his hands, surrounded by sympathetic camera men and production assistants.

Samantha studied these good people she had become so close to during these last few months. When A.J. had called her into his office, she had expected the proverbial pink slip of dismissal to make way for a younger, blonder newscaster.

Instead, he had produced a bolt-from-the-blue job offer, for not only a night beat-type reporter, but, for a faithful companion........ they wanted Bernie, too!

"This guy, a ....Delbert Lenape, had seen you and Bern, here on a public service announcement and evidently fell in love with both of you! I checked 'em out----googled 'em and this is totally on the up and up. Probably, in 'Joisey' they would say 'legit' Half-way across the country in New Jersey.. little place called Mountain View. Who knew Jersey had mountains? I thought they just had refineries and the Mafia and Bruce Springsteen...... Mountain View, New Jersey?! Please! Turns out....here, look I got it right now," Sam leaned over his shoulder to look at the monitor.

"Look it, it's a train station....'New Jersey Transit '--you can be in Manhattan in fifteen minutes! Wow!

Anyhow, the TV station is in Wayne, N.J., which looks like a nice place, 50,000 people or so...be a lot going on, a fun place to live, I would think. Did I mention? Are you ready? He's got a place for you and your buddy here, to live?! A house with a yard for big boy, here. I can't stand it!

Listen, it's up to you, but you'd be a fool to pass this up. I mean, c'mon! They asked for you, by name, and they want your dog, too, fer cryin' out loud!!! If you don't take this, I'm gonna kidnap Bernie and take it myself!!"

Bernard responded to his name with a stern glance toward A.J. He always positioned himself protectively between Samantha and any male presence.

Sam had never stayed at any one place, ever. Her life thus far, had been a series of foster homes some good, some not so good, and then a scramble for education and employment. She had gathered almost no possessions until Bernard had come into her life.

Even now, the bet was even money as to who owned whom.

Bernard's life had been much more stable than Sam's'. He had been fortunate to have begun his existence as one of six puppies born to an excellent mother who had picked a busy family's backyard in which to begin her labor. The Anderson daughters, all four of them, had assisted in the births while the father of this remarkable family had fixed a bed in the corner of the crowded garage for the new additions and when the labor was finally over, helped the proud, exhausted mom and six! new lives to the warm, cozy nook.

At first, the puppies looked like.......puppies....... but time soon proved that 'Daisy', their mommie, a Lab mix had been quite the little slut. Various breeds were represented in size, color, coat. Four little girls and two little boys, the largest being Bernard, so named immediately after he opened his eyes.

He grew and grew and grew and grew, never evinced ill temper only calm, protective kindness.

An amalgamation of several large canine breeds (think mastiff, wolfhound, moose) with a smidge of Humvee, Bernie tipped the scales at one hundred fifty, give or take thirty or forty pounds and was furred with masses of fluffy curls, much like an elephantine poodle. He showed an early inclination to protect and be around humans of the female persuasion and when an elderly neighbor obviously needed a dose of chivalry, the Anderson's introduced them.

At once he became Madge's escort and comfort, opening doors, shouldering through crowds, providing a steadying presence, standing guard on the darkest of lonely nights, being her friend. They had almost three happy years together.

But, when Madge's family discovered she had been writing large checks to TV evangelists, buying masses of lottery tickets on her credit card and leaving the back door unlocked so Bernie could come and go as needed, they put Madge into a nursing home and took Bernie to the Humane Society, much against his will.

Homeless, he was grieving mightily, starving himself, when the fateful 'pet o' the week' segment brought he and Sam together.

Samantha, having been more or less homeless all her life, instantly gained her first pet, a staunch protector and true friend. They were never apart.

He now dined exclusively on turkey club sandwiches, hold the tomato and lettuce, and an occasional Miller Lite.

Jaych, during the commercial break patted the distraught Smitty's back awkwardly.

"There, there, we'll keep in touch, it's not good bye, just so long for a while..." "She hates football, can't stand baseball and she's gonna be ten miles from the MEADOWLANDS, GIANT'S STADIUM, and FIFTEEN MILES FROM THE NEW YANKEE'S BALL FIELD!!!! OOOOHHHH, TAKE ME NOW!!!! THERE HAS TO BE SOME MISTAKE!!!! NOT FAIR! NOT FAIR! NO-O-O-O-O-O------!!!!"

Samantha decided to take some time and drive herself and Bernard across the mid-section of the nation, never having taken much time off from her career to enjoy herself. Her yellow Corvette would be a tight squeeze for her best friend, but she was in no hurry and they could just slow down and look the countryside over.

"Whaddya think, Bern? Shall we motor on? Good boy!"

Moving on, changing jobs, changing a life...nothing new for Sam. Change is hardly ever all bad, all good----- just ....change.

Early on, she had learned to precipitate, instigate, and manipulate....change.

Sometimes, just for kicks............ sometimes, just because she could...........

And sometimes, for self-defense.

CHAPTER TWO

Dogs are mentioned fourteen times in the Bible.

Little Sammi Bister did not realize she was a statistic until she had been reading for several years and by that time she knew, if not the pronunciation, the spirit and value of 'manipulation'. Early on she had learned the fine art of a well-placed tearful tale or hysterics or tantrums, or illness.

When she began the third grade (at the third school) a third set of foster parents was re-thinking their commitment.

Seth and Margene Oster had been married for fifteen barren years. Seth's family, initially pleased he was to marry, the war in Vietnam taking it's bloody toll, after the fact began finding fault with Margene and anything to do with Margene.

This was incomprehensible to her. She had never encountered such hostility, even in grade school, well-known hotbed of bullying behavior.

What to do?

Margene cleaned their sad little shabby furnished apartment thoroughly, banishing years of other people's dirt.

Not enough.

She pored over cookbooks, spent hours concocting elaborate meals from the frugal food allowance.

Ridiculed.

She initiated holiday traditions and celebrations.

Scorned.

She cried more in those first two years of what was supposed to be wedded bless than in all the previous eighteen.

She tried not to hate.

Seth's family blamed Margene for the lack of babies (Seth's brothers and sisters being disgustingly fertile) and Margene's family blamed Seth. The pressure from both sides was nearly unbearable.

When Margene's childhood chum, Beth Ann, gained a position with the state office of Child Welfare and mentioned the Foster Care program, it seemed prayers had at last been heard.

Margene wheedled and cajoled and begged Seth, who loved Margene deeply, to consider adoption, or at least a foster care arrangement (which would come with a government check, after all) and he finally relented, overcoming immense pressure from his father who kept up a steady dialog against caring for 'some low-life's damaged brat'.

The paperwork was begun.

For Margene, a new day dawned, birds sang, flowers bloomed at her every step.

Her beloved Seth! At last!

Triumphant, Margene prepared their plain little home (Seth's father did not care for 'pretty') in anticipation of a tiny blessing to fill the empty spot in her heart and life.

A second-hand crib was found for the spare room, which got a fast coat of yellow paint, just to be safe.

She could feel deep in her soul that somewhere out there was a tiny baby boy in desperate need of a loving family and home.

She concentrated on the newborn soon to complete her family. When he arrived she would be fully prepared to be the best mother in history of mom hood.

Yes, she would.

When Sammi Bister, female, ten years old, tear-stained and sullen, walked into the yellow room with hand-hemmed gingham curtains that matched the blankie in the crib, Margene did not flinch.

She took Sammi's hand, told her the crib was for a baby brother soon to come but for now it was the perfect place for Sammi's dollie and she would have a bed of her own just as soon as one could be brought in with whatever color blanket she wanted on it.

Maybe a bright red blankie with pillow to match? "No! Not red!" Sammi shook her head vehemently. "Not red!" But, would Dollie like some new clothes?

And Sammi thought it might work out.

Then Seth's father, suffering from 'little man's syndrome' met Sammi and told Margene to make her a 'decent dress'. He gave quite a lot of orders and strutted some, all the while staring at Sammi, trying to make an impression and get his bluff in on her. Sammi, who had just eaten a very good lunch of spaghetti and meatballs and a chocolate shake, looked at him with eyes that had seen his kind before, and threw all of that good, large lunch, every bit of it, up on his brand new high-heeled ostrich skin cowboy boots.

Immediately, a smiling Margene fixed Sammi a nice warm bubble bath, washed her hair with the best shampoo, dried her in a warm fluffy towel and rocked her until she slept.

When Margene told Seth about the calamitous meeting and the cowboy boots, he laughed until tears ran down his face and she saw the man she had fallen in love with so long ago.

And she thought it might work out.

And very soon, as often happens in these situations, Margene conceived triplets.

Margene and Sammi understood each other very well, each had goals in life, both determined to guide events as much as possible.

The pregnancy gave Margene vastly more influence in familial politics.

Like a bird released from a cage, she surveyed her subjects (Seth and Sammi) and made decisions that had far-reaching results.

Sammi loved Margene and was fascinated by the pregnancy, which became the focus of the Osters'.

She stepped in immediately, helping during the all-day morning sickness, when Seth turned green.

She did household chores more and more when Margene's tummy just got to be too much, and finally, when the expectant mom was confined to bed, she was indispensable.

But, she never took orders from Seth's father.

The triplets, two girls and a boy came into this troubled world at full-term, full-weight, and full-cry.

The proud father, newly self-confident, and assured in his role had become the man Margene had glimpsed at the beginning, and had left his job at his dad's store.

His new career provided a larger home and part-time help for Margene, much to the disapproval of the Osters and to the delight of Sammi and Margene.

Sammi was smitten with the babies, Mary, Jeanie and Samuel. But she felt the difference; keenly........they would always know their parents....

And, when the babies were becoming people in their own right, she called her caseworker and invented an excuse, grabbed her pillowcase, hugged Margene hard, and moved on.

Maybe.........?

CHAPTER THREE

Every year, $1.5 billion is spent on pet food. This is four times the amount spent on baby food.

So, they made pretty good time, just the two of them. A hundred miles or so down the road, Sam eased the 'vette into a lushly wooded area, advertised as a scenic river way and she and Bernie took advantage of the open spaces to stretch their legs and enjoy the freedom. Evidently a fiesta of scents to delight doggy noses was all around them to judges by Bernard's reactions.

He charged here, there, sniffing, dowsing bushes that might catch fire, scratching, barking, joy oozing from every wiggly body part.

She took advantage of his preoccupation and ambled along in his wake, following a graveled path down a precipitous decline, savoring the silence of the deep forest, broken only by the sounds of the dog's crashing in the leaves and squirrels cursing from the tops of ancient oaks.

The clean scent of an occasional pine gave way to a more earthy aroma and the gurgle of running water.

Bernie was mid-way into the river when Sam walked across the gravel bar. His smiling face was all that was visible as he swam to the other side of the swift-flowing stream.

A mental picture of her beloved 'vette's leather seats flashed.....had she brought towels? This trek might take more than the week she had first envisioned at this rate, and it wasn't fair to keep such a large, healthy animal cooped up for a really long amount of time.

"Well, fine!" she reinforced her initial decision. "Let's take out time and enjoy our good luck. OK? Bern? OK?"

He had emerged, fur flattened with water, looking smaller but still huge, at the base of a cliff which dominated the scene.

Sam slipped her shoes off, soon re-learning three (3) rather important lessons: 1. the small rocks beside the water are sharp! 2. Also, hard! And, 3. Water is cold!

Very soon, the shoes were back on the offended feet and she was noticing how the light was changing and the day lengthening.

"OK, Bernie, let's get a move on!"

The climb up the gravel road back to the clearing where the yellow Corvette waited, gleaming in the waning sunlight was refreshing and the friends felt ready to forge ahead.

"What a gorgeous day, Bern! Shall we load 'em up and head on out?" Bernard shook the last few drops from his curls and grinned at her.

So, she grinned back.

He re-established himself in the 'shotgun' position and sighed resignedly.

As she belted herself, Samantha noticed in the weeds along the path, a thorny vine snaking it's way along the rocky ground, culminating in a rather bedraggled pink rose.

Leaning out of the low-slung sports car she picked it.

"Last rose of summer, Bern, just waiting for us. Only, it smells like fall now." He showed polite interest, only, going to sleep almost as soon as Sam had put the rose over the visor and turned the key.

The miles flowed along under the vette's wheels until hunger finally prompted Sam to ask, "How about a snack, Bernie?" This being a rhetorical question, Sam pulled into the drive-thru at the first available fast food joint and placed their order for thirteen grilled turkey sandwiches, twelve plain, one with tomato only and a sweet tea.

After the order was repeated twice, she moved out of the lengthening, honking line.

The clerk/cook/waiter brought the food out to them shortly, staying only long enough to collect payment and watch Bernie eat a few of the sandwiches.

The miles passed quite pleasantly in this fashion across several states. They roomed in very nice dog-friendly accommodations and lunched at road-side restaurants and a memorable sidewalk cafe with wrought iron tables and gourmet menus.

Bernie made friends with the server at first glance and received a lovely *cassole poulet* with subtle but persistent overtones of sage.

She and Sam were enjoying a lovely aperitif of a very unassuming Chablis, when a well dressed man, uninvited, sat at their table, leaned closely into Samantha's comfort zone and said, "I've been watching you all evening, my dear. Are you traveling alone ? May I buy you and your... er...puppy another round? I can't believe someone as lovely as you would be without a man to protect you. Are you a celebrity? You look like a movie star......May I know your name? Are you a singer? You look like someone familiar......."

Bernard rose to his full height and sternly gazed at the interloper and rumbled deeply.

'Romeo' gulped and valiantly tried again.

"Are you a singer? Are you Annette? Annette!!! That's who you are!!!!! Hehehehh heh....... I like dogs.......... hehehe.......Nice boy!"

The 'nice boy' raised his hackles ever so slightly rumbled again and smiled, showing most of his teeth, especially the pointy ones.

Samantha smiled too, as 'Romeo' moved, quickly away.

"You really are a good boy!!! Have some more wine..."

At nearly fifty, Samantha had had an abundance of 'Romeos'. As a foster care recipient/victim, with growing cynicism she had learned certain characteristics to be aware of. Suits and gold chains were warning signals........

Case in point: but much later in our little story, the Midgleys....

CHAPTER FOUR

Dogs have fewer taste buds than people---probably fewer than 2,000. It is the smell that initially attracts them to a particular food.

The Children's Division rule requiring supervisors to make reasonable efforts to report to law authorities when a foster child is a clear threat to another is one of the many subterfuges that Sammi had used several times in her storied career in state care. Case workers meet for emergencies and schedule regular check-ins with clients and families. Sammi, having been in the system for ten or eleven families, realized early on how to use it to her advantage. So, when the Hoppingtons decided to make foster care a career and to make Sammi the work force, she developed a plan.

Sammi was placed with these lovely people, appearing on their doorstep late one spring, clutching the pillowcase containing the evidence of her life so far.

Well-meaning people with the best intentions in the whole wide world, god love 'em and bless 'em, Sammi thought cynically. "What now............"

Pale and forty-ish, Marvin Hoppington loved movies, his wife, and children. He suffered from an assortment of ill-defined maladies which precluded any sort of paid employment, thusly attaining the holy grail of 'disability checks'.

Cecelia Hoppington loved her Marvin, movies and anything baked in the ovens of 'Little Debbie'. Cecelia had never attained her high school diploma and perhaps weighed a touch over three hundred pounds.

They had welcomed into their home the first of their foster kids, Richard, who at four was proving to be a bit more than they had bargained for. Maybe, they thought, he would be more content with a 'sibling' closed to his own age...maybe an older child to occupy him and perhaps help out?

Richard did not seem to care much for movies unless they were cartoons which Marvin did not like at all, being more into war movies, which gave Richard night frights.

Enter Sammi, ten years old, tall for her years, system-jaded far beyond.

"Sammi Bister! What a pretty name and what a pretty young lady you are! I am Cecelia and this is Marvin. You can call us Mom and Dad if you want and this is your new little brother, Richard Dickerson. Someday, maybe you can both be Hoppingtons, wouldn't that be nice?

Sammi, you are going to have that nice little room by the kitchen.......yes, right there. Sorry, no window....I think it used to be the pantry. Just put your, er, bag in there, make yourself at home and on your way back in, would you bring another coke for your dad and a coupla' of those carrot cakes for me, what a good little helper you are! Help yourself to what ever you want and bring something for Bubby, too."

In anticipation of the check from Family Services, the Hoppingtons had purchased, on time, the biggest T.V./V.C.R. combo on the market. The convenience store down the street had a never-ending supply of movies for rent conveniently displayed near the check-out.

Of course, the tragedies of many American families, poverty, drugs and illness made for a glut of potential foster children and all those lovely checks from the government.

The Hoppingtons, in the fervor of doing good, brought on by those lovely checks, saw a rosy future.

Sammi regarded Richard with distaste. His only interest was the soft drink and the snack cake she proffered.

The fact that he was attired in a bright red t-shirt did not endear him to her.

They did not speak, then or in the next three years, as four additional 'brothers and sisters' were welcomed into Marvin and Cecelia's shabby little house: Mickey Smurtz, six and a half, La Shanda Washington, eight, Jonathan Nikkelson, three, and Kathy Lee Effinham, six months.

Someone was always sick or crying or both. Nothing was ever really clean. And Sammi was the only one who cared.

She grew to hate the battered automatic clothes washer that lurked in a kitchen closet along with the canned goods. Before school, Sammi was expected to put a load of dirty clothes in while she munched on a quick breakfast of toast and juice.

The Hoppingtons usually remained abed until noonish. Richard and the other assorted children roamed around the cluttered little hovel, grazing on cold cereal and soda-pop, watching cartoons, all day.

When Sammi returned from a day of classes, she cleared the chaos from the kitchen, carrying snacks to Marvin and Cecelia and what ever child was with them in front of the T.V., while they were mired in some movie plot or another.

Before going to her room for the night, she transferred the wet clothes that were still in the washer to the dryer and clicked the controls so it would do it's work while the household was asleep. The sheer dreariness of this cramped life was exhausting.

Sammi decided, early on, that she did NOT want to become a Hoppington.

So, she plotted her escape.

One bright Monday morning, a wiser Sammi Bister, before leaving for school, placed all the Little Debbie snack cakes and cookies, wrappers included, a brand-new, bright red tee-shirt, all of Marvin's white boxers and Cecelia's white sweater, into the well-used automatic washer, along with an entire bottle of dish washing liquid, set the controls for HEAVY DUTY, HOT, ON.

She called her case-worker, grabbed her precious pillow case, closed the door softly behind her (the Hoppintons were late sleepers) and caught the school bus, stepping out of the frying pan and firmly into the fire.

CHAPTER FIVE

In 17ᵗʰ Century England, during heavy downpours many poor cats and dogs unfortunately drowned and their bodies would be seen floating in the rain torrents that raced through the streets, giving us the expression 'raining cats and dogs.'

The cramped Corvette interior stunk of wet dog. Samantha adjusted the air conditioner again in hopes of clearing the windshield's inner moisture. Passing signs assured her that Interstate 70 was the path to Columbus, Ohio, and that gas and eats would be within her grasp quite soon. The truck ahead was throwing so much water up from the pavement, Sam let the 'vette back off a few miles to be safer.

She had followed this same tractor-trailer through much of Indiana. At the rest stop some miles back, she and the driver had struck up a conversation about dogs, in general and in particular. His traveling companion was a white, bossy Chihuahua, named 'Belle'.

"Really the wife's dog, she's at her mother's. Her mother hates dogs and hates me so, me and Belle are making the run to Wheeling, W. Virginia, on our own. Whereabouts are you and Bernard headed? New Jersey? Listen, you wouldn't believe it, just from the news and stuff, but it's really pretty up in there.....well, they call it the Garden State....I thought that was just sort of slam, you know, kind of back handed like, but it's real nice. Lots of people, though.....

I get into Newark now and then. See, if I work it just right, I can have a lay-over and catch a game....I can generally work it just right........

Well, this ain't making any miles....

You take care, now.....there's another road side park just past Columbus that's real handy, just in case one of you might need one." He looked significantly at Bernie. "Take care now....Nice talking to ya!"

Sam followed his leadership out onto the busy four-lane and together they navigated the tricky ramps and lane changes, past the Capitol building and the German village, Sam concentrating mightily.

The Blacklick Woods Metro park looked inviting to both travelers after more miles and more rain.

Thankfully, Sam pulled the yellow 'vette into the parking lot near the facilities and Bernard, spying trees and grass, bounded away, leaving Sam to her own devices.

She hoped for the best, just please, NOT in the foot path!

Emerging refreshed from the comfort station, she was greeted by a distraught park ranger and an equally upset Bernard.

"Madame, are you the owner of this, this ...DOG? He is NOT leashed and he has committed an OUTRAGE in this public park and he has threatened me!"

Bernie nudged Samantha's shoulder and licked her ear....

"Oh, Captain! I am so sorry! We have been on the road so-o-o long and when we came upon this beautiful place I'm afraid we were both so desperate for......'er relief!...

My apologies, Sir! What can I do to make this right, Major? My friend, Bernard, here, apologizes also... NEVER have done such a thing if he had not been in dire straits......Can I pay for the damages? Bernie, here is my closest companion and, of course, I take full responsibility, General."

Sensing tension, Bernard offered his paw to the ranger who flinched and would have fallen if it had not been for his shovel

"Ma'am, our rules clearly state all.....manure from pets must be collected in an approved bag and placed in a dumpster or removed from the premises."

"And quite right, too, Admiral. We must have standards! Bernard must have been very uncomfortable to have lost control. He feels just awful about this, I'm sure. Don't you, Bernie?"

Bernie smiled even more, (some might mistake it for a snarl) and offered his other, massive paw.

"Well, I guess I could........," the ranger began.

"THANK you, SO much, your honor! Of course, we will make a monetary donation to this lovely place. Thank you! So much! Bernard and I appreciate this more than we can express!

You have our solemn promise this will NEVER happen, ever again!"

Sam pressed a bill into the officer's hand and she and Bernie practiced their quick escape act and were out of the park and back on the interstate very expeditiously.

At a Zanesville drive-thru fast food joint, they had the usual (fifteen plain turkey sandwiches, one with tomato, four waters), inquired about dog-friendly lodgings, where they watched wildlife T.V. shows until very late.......

CHAPTER SIX

39 percent of pet owners say they have more photos of their pet than their spouse or significant other. Only 21 percent have more pictures of their spouse or significant other than their pet.

Nearly overwhelmed, the family court system tries, in it's cumbersome governmental way to bring permanence to children orphaned by any number of circumstances. The court assumes that everyone is working in good faith to this end, and in the vast majority of these cases, success is achieved. Tragedies turned into bliss, families are created from what was an abyss of neglect and abuse.

That, of course, is the hoped-for result. Sometimes, though, personal gain rears it's ugly, egotistical head.

When Sammi Bister came to live at the Midgley's at the difficult age of fifteen, she was past any such hope. But, the Midgleys were not.

Dwayne Midgley had planned his life. He wasn't going to waste one instant of his life. He was going places.

The highest.

The long years of law school had finally paid off and he had attained his goal of partnership in the law firm of Farber, Billingsley, Goldstein and Boggs, when Wade Billingsley had knocked himself unconscious when he slipped in the tub and subsequently drowned last June.

A step up.

Dwayne belonged to a number of civic and charitable organizations.

Climbing..........climbing.

He had acquired a proper sized home in a proper neighbor hood.

Higher.......

He married Justine Johnson, the former Miss Adair County, a work of art.

Think "trophy wife".

Beauty is not always a blessing, often being a either a crutch or conversely, a burden.

Justine worked at her looks all her life: Butter never crossed her lips. Bread, red meat, forbidden. Only chicken, poached. Fruits and vegetables, and very few of those, resulting in constant hunger, but a constant size '6'.

The hair took hours-------color, alone required a degree in chemistry, but the results were a marvel. The cut, the styling, to spray or not. Gel? Mousse? What shampoo?

The Pentagon might have more decisions-------maybe.

Perfume? Well, goodness! One can't just go down to the corner drugstore and pick it off the shelf!

Clothes?

She had a lady who was a genius with fabric and style and hue, and tone and fit and hems and such.

Such a perfectionist!

Her very favorite color was red.

Justine had a goal, too.

Marry well, to an ambitious man.

Her goal and Dwayne's plan meshed quite well. She made sure she was at the right party at the right time.

Bingo!

But after the goal had been achieved, the thrill of the hunt and the conquest, the everyday realities set in and Justine realized she was lonely in the obligatory big house in the 'right' neighborhood and thought it might be fun to have a 'little sister' to play dress-up with and to go shopping with and display.

Dwayne thought it might be a boost for his political career to be seen as an advocate of the Social Services, and the Family Court and the notoriously under-funded foster care system.

So, strings were pulled, money found the right pocket, and Justine had her companion.

Sammi took a look around her at the ostentatious home, and at pampered Justine, and wondered what was in store for her, this time.....

Justine told her all about the glamour of beauty pageants, and all the secrets of the beauty pageant business and they went shopping and played with make-up and nail polish and their hair, goodness, their hair!

Sammi felt she had stumbled into a wonderland of self-indulgence: never before in her life had she experienced this level of personal attention. Justine spared no expense in spoiling her new protégée'/child or for that matter, herself.

And soon the pair looked nearly the same.

But, Sammi never wore red lipstick or the red dress that was especially made.

And soon, Dwayne, who liked pretty things in general and pretty female things in particular, noticed Sammi.

And suggested they go for a little ride in his new car.

Just the two of them.

And Justine noticed Dwayne noticing Sammi, cut the zippers out of all his dress pants, even the Armani suit pants and slapped Sammi and called her a very bad name. When Dwayne came home from his day at the office, she threw an entire set of Noritake china, serving pieces and all, at his head, drove the Porsche to the First National Bank where she drained the joint accounts, before ramming that same Porsche that Dwayne had wanted to take Sammi for a ride in, repeatedly into the retaining wall down at the park.

Sammi, who decided a plan of action rather quickly, first called the police station, then her beleaguered case worker, Ermmaline McQuine, who easily put her hands on Sammi's file, which was the thickness of a medium-sized city's phone book, and said "I'm on my way, baby".

When the police responded, Sammi told the whole story, neatly ending Dwayne's political career before it even drew breath.

She also decided to be "Samantha" from now on and Ermmaline said "Here we go again, but did I tell you about the budget cuts?" and they left a dazed Dwayne with the cops and the mess.

CHAPTER SEVEN

An estimated 1mllion dogs in the United States have been named the primary beneficiary in their owner's will.

"Will you DO something about your mother!!? Anthony, she's nuts and she's driving me nuts, This is beyond creepy, this can't be healthy, Anthony. Will you just look at that!?"

Patty waved her hand upwards, Vanna White-ishly....

"What're we doing with a wedding portrait of Annette Funicello over the mantle, Patty? I mean, I never say anything 'bout what you do with the house, but don't go blaming my mother for this! She's a just little old lady, for crying out loud! She didn't do this; she's only four feet nine. It's you, Patty, you never liked my mother............ but,.............this! Ohhhh,......... Patty!"

Patty pointed her finger up the stairs, Vanna, again.

"Your son! Your mother has corrupted Nikko! They're thick as thieves. She paid him five dollars to take down our family portrait we paid fifteen hundred dollars to have your cousin paint in oils while he was in rehab after he got out of the federal pen. Well, I never liked how he did my eyes, but, still, it was a perfectly nice FAMILY portrait. This is just sick, Anthony! You gotta do something!"

"What am I missing here, Patty? To what purpose would a old lady put a wedding picture of Annette Funicello on the wall? Please fill me in...."

"It's your SISTER, Anthony! Your long lost sister Nicci!! She never talks about anything else, your mother! For god's sake, Anthony! Where have you been for the last forty plus years, Anthony!?"

Angelina Buongiovanni had lived with her oldest son and his family (wife, Patty, grandson Nikko, granddaughter, Aida Marie) for forty long years after Anthony, Sr., had been murdered while working on the docks. The police had considered the crime a 'contract killing' and thusly none of their business, so it was never solved.

Angelina had felt the sudden loss of her husband keenly, but the long-ago theft of little Nicci and the anger directed at her one-time best friend Renae Amortuzzio, the thief, had sustained her for these long decades.

. She obsessed over the daughter so cruelly snatched from her arms and never gave up hope of little Nicci's return, and pestered Tony, Sr.s' comrades to put out feelers to 'get' Gianni Moreno and Renae.

There had been no official investigations for obvious reasons. The 'organization' took care of it's own. Arms were twisted, legs broken, fingers trimmed, assorted vandalisms perpetrated by a couple of Tony's friends (some would refer to them as 'goons) who had almost certainly tracked the kidnappers to Newark, but that was way back then........and since that glimmer of hope, nothing.

And, time passed.

Angelina thought about her lost baby night and day. Family, friends and unsuspecting strangers on the street and in waiting rooms, within minutes learned all about Nicci and the awful circumstances of her tragic disappearance. She searched newspapers, never missed the nightly news. When the airwaves were permeated with cold case-type dramas, she became an instant fanatic. True forensic programs provided her with hope and something to hang onto in the sleepless, dark, early-morning chill.

So, when little Suzy Howderschell, ten years old, pretty and blond, disappeared on her way home from school on a bright October morning, Angelina soaked up the details of the search and the sad vigils like a sponge that had been born in Death Valley.

Suzy's desperate parents contacted the authorities immediately. Search parties covered the area looking under every leaf, rock, scrap of trash; ponds were drained, bloodhounds were brought in, to no happy outcome.

Months turned into years, hopes, once impossibly lofty, became lower than the lowest.

The Howderschells wondered to themselves how Suzy might have looked as she grew into a teenager, and a college-bound student, a cheer leader, a bride.

Never once did they allow themselves to contemplate the probable, ugly, brutal fate of their little girl.

On each anniversary of the last day they had of Suzy, they contacted the police, who having nothing else to offer, suggested the interesting technique of age-progression photography. The Howderschells were comforted by the images of Suzy as a pretty sixteen year-old, a graduate, complete with cap and gown, a bridesmaid.

Television news programs featured these weird photos, asking for tips and information at the anniversaries of Suzy's disappearance.

Little Suzy's fate remained a mystery. Sadly, the 'photos' of a never-never life were all her parents ever had of her, ever, and they clung to them.

"Fast Forward Friendly Photographer, Fran speaking, how can we help?"

"Hello? I saw you on the television, are you the ones that do pictures of people that are missing? Like how they would look now?"

"We can rewind, we can fast forward, we can bring your great-grandmother back to life, we can..........."

"My Nicci was stolen from me when she was two years old by that bitch Renae Amortuzzio and that no-good Gianni Moreno....they ran away and took my Nicci!! My Nicci will be fifty years old on her birthday this year and

I never got to see her grow up! My life was ruined! She would have taken care of me. Now I have to live with my son and that woman he married. If only Nicci...."

"So, Mrs.?.........If you would just bring your picture album in and the last picture you have of .....Nicci?...I'm sure we can help you see her as she would be today...if she hadn't been k.k.k......mur.....stolen!"

"My Nicci lives! A mother knows these things! Don't you ever think different! Nicci lives! She is probably married with babies of her own! And grand babies! My great-grandchildren! Can you make pictures of my great-grand babies?"

Fran, sensing the warm, golden glow of job security, in her most sympathetic voice answered, "Of course, we can, Mrs......? We'll bring you up to-date with Nicci. We make sure that families never miss out on the important parts of the loved one's......life. If I could just have your name, Mrs.?...."

"My Anthony was taken from me years ago and now I have to live with Anthony, Jr. and that woman he married. She hates me. But my grandson Nikko is the light of my life!. He is......."

"They sound like lovely people, Mrs'?......?

"Anthony Boungiovanni, Senior! My Anthony was a strong, working man down on the docks. Maybe you've heard of him...?"

Fran had indeed heard of him. More familiarly know as 'Snickers' for the joy he had gotten from killing and for his candy bar of choice, Anthony's demise in the not-too distant past by persons unknown, had brought joy and relief to all levels of the population of Weehawken.

"Ahh....Mrs. Boungiovanni! Of course, I've heard of your family! As a courtesy, we'll send a messenger right over to pick up your information. All we need is your photo album and a good picture of your....Nicci...We'll fix you right up. Nice talking to ya...."

As Angelina listened to her son and Patty arguing downstairs about Nicci's lovely wedding portrait, she looked through her brand-new album, delivered this morning. It was thrilling to see Nicci as college grad, Nicci as Miss New Jersey, Nicci as new mother-to-be..... her babies.......

CHAPTER EIGHT

Seventy percent of people sign their dog's name on greeting cards and fifty-eight percent include their pets in family and holiday portraits.

"Yeah, I can hear you........................No, we're fine, yeah, someplace in Pennsylvania......No, we're in a wayside park, Yeah, Bernie is fine as long as he gets to go out in some trees and grass.............."

Sam had finally realized what that annoyingly persistent buzzing racket was and found the appropriate button and magically heard Jaych's voice. The gang at the station, fearing she would never call them, had chipped in for a cell phone, plus contract plus instructions and advice. She had been on her own, alone but not lonely for a good long bit, and while the heart-felt solicitude of her co-workers was comforting, it was also a little overwhelming.

Sam had promptly turned the tiny contraption to what she mistakenly thought of as the 'off' position and was, in fact, 'vibrate'. Assuming the intermittent hum was a 'Chevy noise' and since the Corvette still ate up the miles, she and Bernie had motored on.

"Yeah, I think we'll get to Mtn. View in the morning. We'll stay around Harrisburg tonight and get an early start tomorrow. I don't want to try to find the place in the dark...."

Jaych cautioned, "Well, just be aware of black widow spider and brown recluse. Usually, they wouldn't dream of bothering you but in case the former tenants didn't clean well, just keep a watch out for 'em. I showed you the pictures, remember?"

Jaych went on: "I'm glad you're thinking ahead and will have daylight on your side. Did you do a map quest or Google your new address? Wayne? I thought you were going to Mtn View........"

"Well, that's a New Jersey Transit station.......I guess a commuter line......Yeah, way different...." Jaych preached on: "Listen, It looks like on the radar that the weather is in the control of a powerful high-pressure system and should remain clear and dry for a week or so...And, listen, be sure and look Bernie over for ticks and don't let him get in the poison ivy........He'll bring all that in with him and contaminate your car or house".

"Oh, my! ......your signal is getting weak....I can hardly hear...............I just get a word now and ....Oh, wow! We're going through a tunnel.........."

Sam firmly switched the little gadget off, closed the case, stowed it back under the front seat and tooted the horn, twice. She was just finishing the chore of getting the roof panel put away (clear skies) when the sound of a fast approaching horse or moose signaled Bernard's return. He rushed to Sam's side to make sure she was safe, then watered all the tires and leaped, relieved into the Corvette's driver's seat and grinned happily.

"Scootch over, let me drive this time."

As they pulled out on HWY 78, Samantha couldn't resist barking the tires, just a little. Bernie smiled at the wind blowing in his curly fur and Sam enjoyed the freshness of the fall air rushing through her curls, too. They had settled down to a steady pace, three miles over the speed limit when a Highway Patrol car pulled even with the Corvette on the inside lane. Bernie and Samantha smiled at the handsome young trooper. He smiled in return and mouthed "Nice car!" Sam waved and gave the thumbs up sign and said 'Thanks!" They kept company for a few miles then his emergency lights flashed on and he accelerated away.

"Good boy, Bernie! You showed him! He knows you would have beaten him in a fair fight!"

She reflected on all the good advice her well-meaning friend had given her. It was comforting to have people concerned with your happiness and well-being. Jaych had a real fascination for spiders and their ilk and considered them her friends.

But, usually, Sam just smashed bugs with her shoe.

A new home, a new life awaited them one hundred miles or so on this busy highway. So many new beginnings in Samantha Bister's life and career. Maybe this new chapter would be the one that filled that empty spot inside. Her friends all knew where they came from, who they were, a sense of history, family.........

Reaching over to touch Bernie's warm, adoring face, she murmured, "Best friend in the world, pal. All I need."

CHAPTER NINE

Most pet owners (94 percent) say their pet makes them smile more than once a day.

Roll call began in Mr. MacAfee's eleventh grade English class:

"Mary Adams"

"Present."

" Jeanne Allan"

"Present".

"Michael Atkinson"

"Here".

"Leanna Barclay"

"Present".

"Samantha Bister"

"Present ".

Raymond MacAfee, in the next-to-last year of his teaching career was trying with the utmost of his burnt-out soul to find even the tiniest glimmer of originality or talent or competence, or hope, in the essays of his students.

Those in the profession of education are among the first of us to recognize the deterioration of society and the realization of this immutable fact leads to thoughts of retirement as soon as practical. The tendency of the voting public to generally vote against any increase in funding for education and wildly in favor of any prison, leads credence to the motto, "Bye, Bye, Baby, Bye, Bye."

"John Grindstaff"
"Present".
"Marvin Haywood".
"Accounted for."
"We are grateful, Mr. Haywood. Megan Joachim?"
"Here, sir!"
"Thank you, Megan, Angela Leonetti?...Angela?"
"Louise Martin"
"Present, Mr. MacAfee."
"Delighted, Miss Martin"
"Deliver me, please, Great Professor in the Sky from these girl hood crushes"

Eventually, the body of the class began. Today's assignment was to read the essays that the student had written about any subject of the student's choosing....

Mr. MacAfee's assignment was to not grimace or show any impatience or to ridicule any of this crop of tomorrow's leaders.

Raymond called for volunteers to begin and prepared himself with a suitably expectant facial expression. Predictably, Heather McIntyre began and went over the allotted five minute limit, droning on about world peace and working herself up into near-hysteria.

"Very nice, Heather. Interesting concept.......I'm sure the world leaders will be overwhelmed to receive your...er...insights........There...there....We can only do so much from our classrooms, Heather. Deep breaths, now...relax....try not to cry.......Well done Heather, thank you....Maybe something lighter for our next essay? O.K., who wants to be next.........,Mary Jane? Very good! Now let's remember and keep an eye on the clock, O.K.? Mary Jane? Let's begin.....

Raymond did not laugh out loud at even the most ridiculous of this half-baked nonsense. All the day long...It took super human powers the likes of which Batman and the Hulk would shrink from like little girls.

He had a happy, happy place and he went there.

"Samantha Bister? Have you prepared an essay to read today? Would you like to do that now, please? Now class, this will be the last reading for today....We will finish our essays tomorrow and then work on vocabulary Ahhhhh...Samantha........you may begin, now."

"I was seventeen years old on Halloween. Every year that is my party....Lucky me! All of you in this classroom know who you are; your families are all around you. My family is the Foster Care system and I have lots of moms and dads and brothers and sisters, but, I never knew my real ones. I have lived in lots of different houses. Some were real nice and some were not but, at each place I learned some things.

At one place, I found out that I do not really like small children much. At another, I learned that just because a person is religious, it doesn't necessarily mean that person is kind or nice.

Lately, I found out how to prepare myself for beauty pageants. See? Just the tips of my hair are still that color. Blonds do NOT have more fun! You just have to work a lot harder to prove that you're not dumb.

The State pays my moms and dads to take care of me. Most of my families really wanted to help me grow up safe and well and I am so grateful to them. But, some of them didn't care about me, all they cared about was the money they got for giving me a place to live. I always felt that there must be something more about me that I should know, but I'm not sure where to begin.

I think my life is going to work out. I hope so I have an afternoon job at the library, but sometimes it seems the money runs out really soon. I will 'age out' next year and I will be on my own.

I plan to go to college so I need to do really well so I can get a scholarship. But, I have moved so many times that my credits sometimes don't count at the next place where I go to school. I hope I can graduate next year and I hope I don't have to move too many more times. But, sometimes things happen and I have to.

But, I know for sure that every year at Halloween there will be a party! Lucky me!"

After the last student hurried from the classroom, after all the chatter died out in the halls, Raymond snapped the fluorescent light off, the buzz stopped and the roar of the traffic in the streets outside was a muted hum.

He sat in the dark, and thought about the years ahead. "Lucky me."

****

Samantha left school, walking quickly downtown the several blocks to the regional library where she had been working for a few hours after classes a couple of days a week.

She liked most of the staff and enjoyed her assignments, mostly shelving books and finding books that various patrons had requested. She often came here to study in a quieter place and had applied for the job when it became available.

As headquarters for the regional library system, the facility was a large rather new building, with areas set aside for study, reading and research. The bathrooms were large and clean, considering they were in a public building.

A couch was positioned near magazine racks, which were kept stocked with various news and entertainment publications, kept up to date, by Sam.

One of the perks of the part-time position was a key to the facility, since often Samantha closed up on the evenings she worked the expanded hours once a week.

Samantha lived at the library sleeping on the couch, doing laundry in the bathroom sink, heating snacks in the microwave several months before anyone was aware. It was the happiest and safest she had ever been.

Take that, budget cuts!

CHAPTER TEN

Dogs can hear sounds that are too faint for us to hear, and also hear noises at a much higher frequency than we can. Their hearing is so good they probably rely more on sound than on sight to navigate their world.

Bernard, sleeping deeply on the double bed nearest the door, emitted little yips, his legs jerking and twitching as outside, the skies over Harrisburg lightened.

Sam kept her eyes closed for just a bit before facing the day, So often, in her childhood, it had behooved her to not advertise her consciousness immediately.

Bernie snored on, in his own doggy world, protecting dream damsels and exploring woodlands and dowsing potential burning bushes.

One more day on the road. They should be in their new home in just a matter of a few hours. The station manager had made the living arrangements for his latest employees. Bernie would have a park and golf course nearby, for his special needs.

Delbert Lenape was confident that the new duo, Samantha and Bernard, 'night beat on the mean streets' of Passaic County, New Jersey would be an instant sensation and, finally, he, Delbert Lenape would be taken seriously in the cruel broadcasting world.

The rank odor of the terrified bison herd as they stampeded over boulders and ravines assailed Bernard's flaring nostrils along with the power-giving oxygen his sinewy muscles craved. Close behind were his starving canine kin in full, blood-thirsty cry, the specter of the cold, hungry starving, dying times driving the pack on.

His mighty, slavering jaws snapped at the plump haunches of the eye-rolling cow as she stumbled, shattering a fragile leg, her tender underbelly, the hot, spurting blood, the succulent liver, the still- beating heart....

"What a wonder puppy you are, Bernie!!!! Time to get going, sweet boy......Rise and shine! You'll have your very own wilderness in just a little while....How do you feel about yummy chicken sandwich or twelve? Goodness! Were you about to catch a dream bunny? Well, you just wait! We're gonna go chase the bad guys all over New Jersey!

Sam attached his leash and he slipped out the door while she checked the room one more time. They traveled light and kept clutter to a minimum so these final sweeps didn't take long. She grabbed her overnighter and went out.

"Nice doggy Nice doggy!......Miss, is this your dog? Please, Miss, I was just checking your tires on your pretty car, Miss! Nice doggy!!!!Miss, Please!!!! Those nuts looked loose to me and I was just checking, Miss!!!! Please!!!! Help!!!! He's going to hurt me!!!!Miss I'll put these back on SO good, Miss!!! Please! Good Dog!!!! Good Boy!!!! Help me!!!!Miss?!!!!!"

The Corvette was parked just outside the motel door, Bernie was 'smiling' at a young fellow who was trying to melt into the brick wall. Lug nuts sparkled in the early morning sun, scattered on the asphalt.

"Miss? Is he your dog? Please, Miss, Help me please! Look, I'm tightenin' 'em up real good, Miss!! Good Dog! AAAAAAAH!!! Is he going to bite? Miss, please...Look! I've got 'em all on!!!!! Could you just please make him..... AAAAAAH!!! Is he going to.......?!!!!"

"Easy, Bernie," She hoped she sounded authoritative and stern. Bernie turned his massive head to gaze adoringly at her as she picked up the end of his yellow (of course) leash, and the frightened young man vanished like smoke.

The miles flowed under those wheels from Pennsylvania to the ever- more congested roadways toward the nation's 'big cities'. Sam was irrationally disappointed when the state lines were announced by roadside signs and rest stops rather than a bold blue speed-bump line like on the maps. Bummer!

Historic monuments and markers increased exponentially until they were nearly touching sides. George Washington, evidently slept nearly everywhere. And , just as advertised, New Jersey, did indeed have mountains...who knew? Interstate 178 exited onto 287 and became more northerly and busier.

287, a very busy interstate, multi-laned and nervous-making for the Midwesterners, carried Sam and Bernie quickly onward, past strange sounding names: Peapack, Pohatcong, Towaco, Parsippany.

"Must have been some wars fought around here, Bern," Sam told her best friend.

At the next rest stop she studied the map and prepared to make the transition to highway #202. Highway signs had been touting the wonders of Boon ton, the 'Home of the world famous 'Boontonware' for miles, so curiosity prevailed and Samantha made a complicated maneuver she would never have had the nerve to attempt two weeks before, and they took a break.

They were both pretty sick of the sports car and the trip was nearly over.....live a little, so what.........

"What a beautiful place, like a post card.....Church steeples, bright leaves....this is gorgeous. If Wayne is half as nice as this, Bern, we have stepped in something very nice. And only ten miles from Manhattan? Crazy, huh.............?!"

They drew attention as they strolled about the pretty town. It felt wonderful to be so near the end of a long, introspective journey. Bernie explored the park of Lord Grace, and Sam struck up conversations with fellow strollers, pronouncing both 'en's' of 'Boon ton', and she was quickly, politely corrected. Turns out, 'Boo'n' is preferred.

After an hour or so of goofing off, they returned to the mobile, yellow prison to finish the task at hand.

Samantha's neck ached with the tension of watching her speed and avoiding the ubiquitous tractor-trailers hauling who-knows-what.

"Just a tiny bit more now, Bernie! There's our sign!"

CHAPTER ELEVEN...

Researchers studying what dogs like to eat have found that the appetite of the dog is affected by the taste, texture and smell of the food and also by the owner's food preferences, their perception of their pet, and the physical environment in which the dog is eating.

"O.K., we're looking for number sixteen........Gee, what a swanky neighborhood, Bernie. Beats our old apartment, huh, puppy.........

Mr. Lenape said it was a nice house with a yard for you and a lot of room inside for me. You know what, sweet friend? We are going the wrong way or else the numbers are going the wrong way, we better turn around, I guess I should'a let you drive........"

This was definitely a step up, very nice homes, split-level, large lots, well maintained, no cars parked on the streets, lush lawns with healthy shrubs and trees.

And then...........yellow ribbons.........yellow welcome signs........ and a yellow sweat-shirted kid energetically attacking a drum set, an older man tootling on a trumpet and a short, dark man in a wrinkled suit who waved them to the road side.

Delbert clutched Sam's hand as she struggled from the Corvette.

"Wayne, New Jersey, welcomes you, Samantha and Bernard".

He looked at a crumpled paper scrap.

"And our television viewing public awaits your professionalism in matters of Crime." Bernie, in protection mode, had at first sniff detected absolutely no threat in Delbert, at all. None. The drummer, who persisted in his efforts, likewise seemed harmless, if noise some.

And the trumpeter was at the moment leaning against a tree and emptying the spit valve and wheezing.

"Ya o.k., Pa? Jeeze louise, Mikee, shaddup! Enough already! "Anyway, welcome! We fixed you a party so you'd feel at home. Ma and my wife, Lola been cooking for days now. I hope ya like it.

Come on in now to your new home. Pay no attention to those ' for sale' signs, my brother-in-law has the listing on this, but nobody's looked at it since......er....since........ er...."

They followed Delbert into the foyer along with the musicians, Mikee supporting Pa who seemed near coma.

The aromatic perfume of roasting garlic and tomato sauce with basil nearly brought the travelers whimpering, to their knees.

"Ah, Ma! This is Samantha Bister and her partner, Bernard. This is my Mother and Lola"

The two women were frozen in place in the kitchen while being investigated by a very hungry canine. Neither of them seemed to breathe.

"Hi! This all smells and looks wonderful! Bernie and I have been living on junk food for the last few days, seems like forever. You are so kind to go to all this trouble for us.

"Bernie, be sweet, now! Good boy!"

'Ma 'and Lola, both rotund and quite challenged height-wise, at last released that last startled gasp of oxygen.

"Ahh! Thank god! We thought it was a bear! Didn't you think it was a bear, Ma? I thought it was a bear! The Montesquieu's had a bear in their yard last week and I thought this was a bear! My god! I thought it was a bear! Scared the life outta me! I thought it was a bear! Didn't you think it was a bear, Ma? I thought for sure it was a bear!"

"Hush, Lola! Jeeze louise! That's enough! Now, Samantha, you guys just make yourselves at home, now... The place is furnished just like they left it that last day.... er....er...........anyway, we painted and replaced the carpet... er...er............ you know...............those stains just wouldn't er...er.........."

Delbert seemed uncomfortable and Lola resumed her monologue.

"So, Samantha Bister, hah? What kinda name izzat? Ya look Italian....Don't she look Italian, Ma? I think she looks Italian....I'm Italian...my whole family is Italian.... Buscoloni is my name....that's Italian. Ma is Indian, right, Ma? Delbert too, of course........ Like redskins, she's Indian. They can go on the warpath, too let me tell you, these Indians do .....Hey, whatzzammata with the dog?!"

Bernie had made a mad dash for the door and was growling deep in his throat. Delbert jerked the heavy door open and screamed out into the street, " Here, you guys! Get away from the car!!!! Get away! Get outta here! Beat it!!! Jeese, I'm sorry Samantha, I never gave it a thought! Ya gotta put your car in the garage all the time. Jeese, I never gave it a thought! Ya got your keys? Good girl!"

Mikee appeared like a bad dream, holding out his rather grungy hand. "I'll park it for ya" "Right in the garage, now Mikee, no speeding now Mikee! He's a good kid, Mikee, good kid. One little scrape, but he's learned his lesson.

I'm watching you, Mikee!

Back in school, now, no problem, good kid."

Lola continued, "I just thought who you look like ..... Annette....Don't she look like Annette, Ma? I think she looks like Annette. She's sick, now, Annette. What's she got, Ma?

Izzit TB?

MS? Ma?

Izzit MS?

Or that ballplayer?

Whats he got? ALS?

Anyway, that's who you look like, Annette Funicello. That's her name...What's you name? Bister? Izzat Italian?

That doesn't sound Italian to me...What kinda name is Bister? Does that sound Italian to you, Ma?"

"Jeese louise, Lola! Hush! Give it a rest, will ya? " We're gonna go now, Samantha. You must be real tired...... we tried to think of everything you might need......If you need any thing at all, you just call. You got our number... you give us a call.

Take your time, now...rest up....take a week....

Take your time and we'll see you at the station in a week on a Monday? O.K.? We'll see ya on a Monday.

You call us for any thing ya need!"

The only sound 'Ma' uttered was as they closed the door behind them.

"Brown...............that's what 'bister' means.....dark brown."

CHAPTER TWELVE

Korea's poshintang-dog meat soup is a popular item on summertime menus, despite outcry from other nations. The soup is believed to cure summer heat ailments, improve male virility, and improve women's complexions.

"Hello?..............Hello?...................Hel...................Hello?.. Jaych?....Hello?................O.K., now I can hear you...can you hear me?.................O.K., there you are!....I just wanted to let you know we got here......Can you hear me?....How about now?...........Yeah, I can hear you.......

Yeah, we got here early this afternoon.....Oh, It's really pretty here, lots of trees and the houses are really classy looking........................

Yeah, we've got a split-level house, three bedrooms, two baths...............yeah, ha, ha, ha, Bernie's got one of his own.........Yeah, yeah, that's funny.............Ha, ha,.............

Well, I guess it's part of my.....our salary. It's been for sale for long time, evidently. Yeah, It's even got sheets and towels and some food in the cabinets. You're tellin' me! This whole deal is unreal......

No, I haven't seen any spiders.....No, I haven't really looked....Yes, I will...............No, I won't.....Yeah I know they are all wonderful and they just wanna be my friends....... I am not!......

Well, I think it's gonna be alright...Every body is really nice so far.....You should have seen all the food his mom and wife fixed for us!!! Yeah, yummy! They had quite a spread fixed when we got here. Yeah, a little party, like...... Yeah, and then they showed me all the stuff they had put in the fridge and the freezer! Bernie is in heaven! I think he has decided to convert and become Italian! Yeah, he's all about the meatballs! He was miserable, he had eaten so much!!! Yeah, me too! It all tasted so-o-o good.......Thank god, there were anti-acids in the medicine cabinet....Yeah, I know! Yeah, it IS kinda weird that everything we need is here, like magic....We walk in...Bingo! Furniture-----food-----appliances------aspirin.... and, I swear, vitamins and Kleenex!

So, how's the gang?........Smitty?.....................Oh, is he still going on about the Meadowlands Sports thingie? Oh, yeah, poor baby.......Yeah, tell him it's even got a horse track and I'm not gonna go to THAT either! And, doesn't Pittsburgh have some kind of ball team? And Philadelphia? And Baltimore ? Well, not gonna go............ Jeese louise!........You're cuttin' out.....What? Can you hear me?......How about now? Yeah, I'm in the back bedroom, now. Yeah, I can hear you fine!......Well, I guess I better go......Yeah, nice to hear your voice, too.....Yeah, well, tell everybody Hi for me.....yeah, I will......Yeah.......talk to ya later.....O.K., Bye......Yeah, bye......."

Sam wandered around in the large, very nice house. So empty, even with all the rather elaborate furniture tastefully arranged. The drapes were obviously custom done and very expensive. Sam had lived in a succession of apartments furnished with hand-me downs and worn out castoffs and had never acquired any thing much of her own. She traveled lightly until Bernard came into her life and he wasn't one to really need too many material things, either.

The rooms opened into each other in a circular way and the excited pair explored every part of the spacious home, for indeed a home it was. Someone had lived here, and cared for all these things, had used this ash tray, had read that book, had replaced it on that shelf, had looked out that window and drawn that curtain.

They wandered on, down a long carpeted hall to a large room with vaulted ceilings and a fireplace, gas logs peeking over the hearth with the obligatory brass tools. Sam noticed the poker missing from the set.

"Probably in the garage. Might have needed to have the ashes knocked off....Oh, look this is where Mikee put the 'vette. I guess everybody has their garage in the back of their house up here....Interesting."

The garage was filled with yard tools, a lawnmower to the side, shelves above, well-filled with miscellaneous boxes, cans, accouterments of home ownership.

Sam and her best friend explored the tiny back yard, which was enclosed with a chain-link fence. The landscaping was professional and very attractive, little thorny bushes of some kind with orange berries. The tall trees were clothed in autumnal fire...red, gold, bronze......

"Just like a pretty jail, Bern. We'll just use it for emergencies, kiddo." They retraced their steps, branching off from the family room to the smaller bedrooms, with beds and dressers and attached bathrooms, beautifully appointed with lush towels and rugs. The pleasant scents of various potpourris arranged in silver bowls here and there added to the aura of the previous inhabitants, who could have just left minutes before, seemingly.

On they wandered, intending on eventually returning to the kitchen with all that lovely food that was NOT a sandwich.

Sam paused at the last door, Bernie close by, as intent on exploration as Columbus. She turned the shiny knob, swung the door into the darkened room, and could go no farther. Bernard stood firmly across the opening.

"Whatsamatter, Bern? Let's go on in and see........" but he wouldn't allow it.

Sam reached in and flipped the wall switch; the lamp on the bedside table came on, revealing a neatly made bed, luxurious spread, matching the drapes. The carpet looked new and untrod upon. A smell of fresh paint wafted out and an odor of another sort.

"This must be the remodeling Delbert was mentioning......Well, it looks nice. Let's go look at the bathroom, Bern, it's probably been redone, too........Aw, come on, I wanna see......Let me in, pal...what's the matter with you?"

But, Bernard, lay down across her way in to the very last room and began to howl.

To those who have never heard the mournful moaning cry of a canine, descriptions are inadequate. Bloodcurdling, spine chilling, lonesome, hopeless, unutterably sad, Bernie was more upset than Sam had ever seen him, and would not be comforted. Only a plate of ravioli, warmed and brought to him persuaded him to leave the doorway. Finally, Sam closed the door to the offending room. Not being a superstitious person, but trusting her best friend's intuition, Sam thought she might have a little talk with her new employer, soon.

CHAPTER THIRTEEN

The last member of the famous Bonaparte family, Jerome Napoleon Bonaparte, died in 1945, of injuries sustained from tripping over the dog's leash.

Delbert ushered the new personalities into the studio.

"Don't pay no attentions to all the real estate signs. My brother-in-law has the listing but who's gonna buy a church, for god's sake.

Now this is where we do our broadcast from. We have local news and then we get a network feed for the national stuff, like you guys did back....where izzit you're from? Montana? Mexico?......Mississippi?....one of them 'M' countries.......Anyway, I guess this is what they call the sanctuary? I dunno, I'm Catholic. The pulpit looks nice on TV, I think! Gives the place a little class."

Sam had driven around Wayne, seemed like a nice place, typical of any town of fifty thousand plus- souls.

Bernard had enjoyed the wind in his face and fur. Sam had stowed the roof panel, the blue skies of late summer demanded to be experienced. The pair in the yellow sports car, with the breezes riffling their dark curls, drew envious glances as they explored the streets of Wayne, looking at what the city had to offer. Neither one of them had ever seen so many people walking around.

Sam slowed for several fast food drive through joints, usually provoking a Pavlovian response in Bernard, but having recently become Italian in persuasion, he only sighed and looked away.

This being the Friday before her first day on the job, following instructions, they were now deep into the tour of the facilities, and being introduced to (it seemed) Delbert's entire family.

"This is Linda Buscoloni, Lola's sister, she's our weather girl.....uh...Meteorologist. She's been off to school and every thing........Linda, this is Samantha Bister and Bernard.......No........NO.....he don't bite!.....Relax!"

"Pleased ta meecha!....How much does your dog weigh? 'Cause he's a really big dog! Lola told me her and Ma though he was a bear, but I knew he wasn't a bear--- Why would a bear be inside? See? I knew he wasn't a bear. What kinda name is 'Blister'? That's not an Italian name, is it? Because you look Italian. Doesn't she look Italian, Del? I think she looks Italian...."

"Give it a rest, Linda!!! Jeez louise! It's 'Bister'.... means 'brown', Ma says it was in some crossword puzzle or something' she was doing'......For cryin' out loud! Why don't you go look at weather or something"?

The sanctuary/studio, complete with piano, choir loft, and pews(looking very 'churchy') having been admired 'enough already', Delbert led on down the hall to the smaller rooms, perhaps classrooms in another incarnation.

Inside one such room, lounging at a battered desk, sat one of the best-looking men Sam had seen in this present life or in of the ones before. Very dark, longish hair, sun-brown complexion, gazing directly into her soul with steady, black eyes, he said something.

Afterwards, Sam only remembered trying to remain standing on her suddenly weakened legs.

"This is my brother, Lenny, short for Leonard. He's the behind-the-scenes guy, runs the sound and tape and stuff. Engineer.......funny, huh? Injun-------engineer-----"

Lenny came to his feet, took Sam's hand in his and said something else.

Later, she hoped she had answered intelligently.......

Then he turned his attention to Bernie, and they communed, probably recalling a past, shared, bloody feast of bison, deep in the primordial ancient forests.

Unaware of any of this soul-searching, communing, tribal stuff, Delbert led on.

Pausing outside the next closed door, Delbert held up his hand like a traffic guard.

"Now, listen....I'm gonna introduce you to my cousin, Floyd Itzinger. He's my own cousin but ya gotta watch him, He's quite the lady-killer, if you know what I mean.....

He's really a smooth talker and he'll charm the pants offa ya. He is the on-air guy, you'll see why in a just a second. We call him Pretty Boy, you know, after the gangster.... get it.....? And he had his moments, but he's turned the corner, now, been straight, now for..............Anyway, sure you're ready? OK, here we go!"

Sam braced herself, wondering if her virtue would survive yet another assault on her senses, as Delbert flung open the door, and all but shouted, "TaDahhhhh!"

"Samantha Bister, this is Floyd Itzinger! And, this is her dog, Bernard. They're gonna do the 'night beat' thing I been telling you about."

Possibly the homeliest man Samantha had ever seen, Floyd oozed upright, slithered around the desk, clutched Sam's hands to his chest and huskily (and with a great deal of garlic) said, "Samantha, my dear! So lovely! So beautiful! *Cara mia!* So charming! So delightful! What can I do to keep you by my side, always?"

Delbert looked on in fascination as Bernie made room between Sam and Floyd for himself. Floyd, who had very tall lifts in his shoes, teetered just a bit.

"Gee! Nice dog........or is he a moose? Good Boy!..... Gosh, he has a lot of teeth, doesn't he? Nice boy!!! Ahhhh.........so soon? Well, I'll keep you in my heart, always.....we'll be together.........This is not goodbye, it's just *ciao*, baby!"

"Really something, ain't he? You can see why he's got all the women falling' all over him, can't ya?" Sam was wondering what it was that she had missed, when sounds of distress or distress erupted from the studio.

Mikee drummed while his clone attacked the piano.

"This here is Mickey, you didn't meet him yet. He and Mikee are twins, I guess I didn't have to tell you, did I? He's doing good with his lessons and sometimes Pop sits in with his trumpet, like if we got a birthday or something patriotic or military....I think it adds a lot, don't you? We're the only live newscast with our own live music in the greater Newark market."

"Listen, Mr. Lenape? I need to ask you a couple of things..........."

"Now, now......we're family,now. No more of this 'mister' stuff.......What do ya need? You running out of food? Do you need clothes? Because I can get ya anything you need, just say the word....no problem....."

"We are fine with everything, er...Delbert, I'm just curious about the back room......the one that's been remodeled?....Is something wrong in there? Bern has a fit every time I try to go in there......"

Delbert quickly pulled her away from the others.

"Listen, you don't need to know anything about that! Just forget it! There's nothing wrong about that room....!"

"But, something is going on..........I...."

"Listen, we got some stuff going on that you don't need to mix in. You not being from the neighborhood, you can't know about this stuff. Just leave it alone..... everything will be fine..."

"Listen, Mr. Lenape, I feel really uncomfortable not knowing........"

"O.K. O.K........we got these.......groups of people that are in.....competition, see? One group hangs out over here, the other hangs out over there, as long as they stay where

they belong everything is fine, if they stray over the line.....
not so much. That's what happened.....somebody strayed
over the line, and the Buongiovanni's took 'em out. Just
don't mix in, O.K.?

OK, then.......we'll see you Monday, OK? You sure
you're OK? Can you drive? If you need any thing, just
call......Anything at all.......

OK, ...O.K.? Seeya Monday!"

CHAPTER FOURTEEN

Before the enactment of the 1978 law that made it mandatory for dog owners in New York City to clean up after their pets, approximately 40 million pounds of dog excrement were deposited on the streets every year.

"..................hope you're happy! Our first day in a new place and and off ya go!..."

The happily exhausted pair was returning from exploring the 'hood'. Nearby TallOaks Park proved delightful and then it seemed to be the thing to do the golf course. Bernie had enthusiastically left a 'deposit' on the fourth green much to the disapproval of a foursome playing through.

Karl and Inge Antonicci, retired and the Krementses, Anton and Millie, turned out to be devoted viewers of the nightly news and were wildly enthusiastic about Bernie's upcoming role on 'night beat', so in the interest of public relations and since it seemed to be *de rigueur*, Sam whipped out the 'doggy doody' bags and cleaned it up.

The likewise named Packanack Lake, reflected the beginnings of fall color from the oaks and maples (more trees!) with waterfront homes as punctuations to the scenic beauty

Sam lengthened her stride and got into her zone. Swinging her arms, out with the bad air, in with the good. Bernard, relieved and lighter now, galloped happily through well-kept yards and fall gardens, scattering the few golden leaves, horrifying some onlookers and enchanting others.

Samantha loved her yellow Corvette, loved the speed, the attention a sports car garnered, had enjoyed the several days she and her best friend had taken to reach this new home. But, even with the roof panel stowed away, even with the early autumn breezes, it had been confining, especially for Bernie. They both had been feeling the need for open space and activity. This morning's exploration was becoming a hike in danger of morphing into a trek, when rounding a brushy corner, Sam spied Bernie and six or seven children in the middle of some sort of hilarious game. As far as anyone could the tell the game involved riding Bernie like a pony and having him wash your face after you fell off. This went on for some time to the vast enjoyment of all. Samantha watched this little festival with a group of moms, who were fans of 'night beat' and thrilled to have met the star. After a bit, Bernie and Sam moved on, promising to come back and play....

She was admiring a rustic sign farther on, Hickory Place, when a she heard a squawk and a shout followed by a splash and more shouting. Following the commotion to lakes edge Sam joined an older couple, dressed alike in matching jogging outfits who were watching a pair of furious swans trying to drown Bernie, who was clambering from the water.

"Nah, he was just playing....he didn't hurt 'em...... they're just touchy and spoiled. Real nice to make your acquaintance....Marge's cousin works at the TV station, so we were pretty sure that was Bernard when we seen 'im, weren't we Marge? The station's been having promos every night for a month, isn't it, Marge?"

Bernard finally reached dry land and hurried out of the reach of the irate birds before shaking the water from his thick fur.

"So, are you guys gonna be neighbors, hah? 'Cause dese streets ain't the mean streets like down town. Nothing happens out here, Dullsville! Baby. Right? Marge? Nothing happens."

"Mr. Lenape has arranged for us to stay for now, back on the other side of the park, Eton court? We needed to stretch our legs this morning so we decided to explore and we just kept going and going and going....."

"Oh, Jeez, you've go a long way to go, let Marge give you a ride in the boat back across the lake. Nah, don't worry 'bout it, she'll let you out on Osbourne terrace, practically back home. She don't mind, do ya, Marge? She don't mind. I gotta stay here to keep Switzer and Heidi from flogging the boat......Seeya on the news!"

Bernard shook again, then he and Sam climbed aboard the tiny fishing boat outfitted (surprise!)with a tiny, nearly silent battery-operated trolling motor. Marge expertly piloted the vessel across the dark, glassy waters

"So, neighbors, hah? I got a sister, Barbie, lives over on Gressinger Road. She grooms dogs in her basement, if you're interested. Himself being a star and all, I thought you might have a need..."

"Well, thanks! I was wondering what to do about getting him all gussied up. He needs to look his best for his debut."

"Yeah, she has a beauty shop, too, if you're interested. She can fix ya both up." Marge gazed at the two disheveled beings in her boat. "If you're interested....So, where did you say you were living? Just asking......"

"Number sixteen, on Eton court. Really nice place, lots of room, nice yard, fully furnished with every thing, I mean, EVERY thing. Even clothes in some of the closets........."

" OH!.....gracious! ....well, uh......... thanks, Marge..... uh.......bye............Marge...."

A suddenly pale and hurried Marge expertly and quickly docked, barely pausing long enough to allow the passengers to disembark before turning and silently retreating back across the still waters.

"Gosh, Bernie! I don't really believe in ghosts, but I think Marge might have just seen one! Hmmmmm...Or maybe she knows what 'group' are the 'bad guys'........... but, we're NOT gonna mix in........

Well, home, boy! How about some ravioli?! Hey! Slow down !........

CHAPTER FIFTEEN

Cats have better memories than dogs. Tests conclude that while a dogs memory lasts no longer than five minutes, a cat's can last as long as 16 hours, exceeding even that of monkeys and orangutans.

"It's her or me!!! I swear, this time is the last-----I've had enough!!! This time I'm the camel's back, with a whole stack of straws....... it's not enough that I have the house, I got your Mother, now it's Halloween, your long-lost sister's birthday, her fiftyith, and it's the blood drive----I'm hearing about this dam' special blood thing, AGAIN!! and STILL she's got all those creepy pictures all over the place...... Nicci, cheer leading....Nicci, graduating from college! Nicci, Queen of the May!!!! I swear, Tony, this is the trifecta of CRAP!!!!!!!

"That dam' blood card came today, that special blood thing, all day, I've heard about how only one per cent of the population has got this blood, and that set her off again! And the mailman says, "OOOH.... Mrs. Buongiovanni, you're one in a million, you are!!!! Popular! Special!" I tellya, Tony, I coulda strangled 'em both!".

Tony Jr. had a strong sense of deja vu. The same scene or one very like it had played out countless times.

"Aw, Patty, I don't know how you do all you do...What smells so good? You've worked all day in the kitchen, haven't you? Here....sit. Let's watch some of the news... and unwind a little....How about just a tiny splash of something....sangria? Yeah, let's....it'll make our dinner taste really nice..no....no...we'll eat when we eat....you don't need to do anything but sit......deep breaths......relax...... whaddya got on here.....what channel?...."

"Oh, Tony, this is fun to watch...They have music during the news...It's from way out in Wayne....nothing ever happens out there, thank god! I cannot imagine...Oh, watch out this...this is cute......they're gonna have a 'night beat' thing on the mean streets ....look it....with a DOG, for cryin' out loud...!

A promo, featuring Bernie's face in close-up, extolling his crime fighting prowess and reminding viewers of the addition to the news team....soon.

"And look at this guy, is that a toupee? Can you believe how ugly this guy is.....? But, funny! Let me just check the oven...I'll be right back....and I think I will have another little splash of wine...You want?.....OK., right back....Listen, thanks, Anthony. I just needed a moment... and a shoulder.....right back."

Tony leaned back on the couch and watched Floyd stumble through the news headlines.

Mean streets! He had had a tense time or two out there in the hinterlands of Wayne, when the cops interrupted just as he and the boys were eliminating some of the competition....Had to be done...messy. Sent a message to the rest of 'em ...if it hadn't been for that park practically next door with all those trees, wilderness, really, could have been a different story.

Oh, the body'll be found some time.........who cares..........They're professionals, they were careful..... As it was, he ruined a nice pair of dress pants on some sort of thorny bushes.. There had been one of those dam chain link fences out back, sure slowed down the escape.

But that garage was a handy thing....private...had a tarp out there and everything And him and the boys had gotten away before the cops had stumbled in.......

Sorta funny.....Wayne cops.....More like Keystone Kops the way they buzzed around looking for the crime.

Patty had raised hell about the slacks.

He wondered idly what had happened to the competition's girl-friend.....I wonder if she's thinks the streets are mean 'way out there in Wayne.......

"Ahh, Patty, here, sit, rest, let's watch the weather.... Listen, don't worry......I'll take ma, just like aways, to go give blood. Then, just like always, we'll go out to the cemetery to dad's grave....

this is what keeps her going. It's been a long time for her to live with this. I've heard about this all my life, I know, I know! Whattya gonna do? Just go on, that's all. That's all you can do. But, you've been great Patty! I know it hasn't been easy, all this time.....

"Oh, look! Drums! Introducing the weather! Wonderful!..... Then we'll eat----I'm starving!....What did you say we're having?"

CHAPTER SIXTEEN

A dog's whiskers are touch-sensitive hairs called vibrasse. They are found on the muzzle, above the eyes and below the jaws and can actually sense tiny changes in airflow.

"So, how do ya want this? Want to keep your length or go shorter? Want a pouffy topknot? Need a little color for those grays?

Yeah, you do.....just a few, not bad yet....but a rinse... a little color.......OK!....OK!....suit your self! There's always next time....

Yeah, I knew who you were when you walked in.....'specially Mr. Dark and Handsome over here..ain't he a love? Yeah, we seen your pictures on the TV.....Crime fighter...hah? Leave it to Delbert to set you up in number sixteen with all that happened there.........................

"Well I can see why he didn't tell ya! Jeez! We watched a lot of it from our front yard. They had the swat team out in full gear--------I don't think I had ever seen so many cops show up so fast!

"Ahh------Delbert's brother-in-law is a low-life......he would like to be connected, if you get my drift, but, listen, honey, ya didn't hear it from me......but he hangs around... doin' favors...you know....I wouldn't want anybody to know I said this but I thing it was a contract.......Yeah, I just BET they put down new carpet-----I just bet!

So, you and Bernie from Montana? Marge said....... Well I thought it was from out that way----

Oh, I wouldn't worry about Bernard.... Bianca'll fix him up-----bath---trim---ribbons in his ears----toenails-----speaking of which, ya wanna get your nails done too? That would be real cute ...You'll match......be a real team.... look good on TV....Impress the bad guys.

OK , OK, Pick a color......

No, I am NOT named after a doll, for cryin' out loud! Do I look like a doll? Don't answer that! No, I like to grill out side...get it? Barbi-----cue? Yeah, I think it's cute---but stupid...but whaddya gonna do----

Yeah, me and the kids do this together...have for years.....Oh, he's one of the bigger ones yeah, but the big ones are usually the sweet ones...It's the poodles that give ya fits......But we have a long list of regulars...What?........... Oh, listen Ben and I have a whaddyacallit......a big Jacuzzi tub and we just give the big boys,like Bernie their bath in that... Ahhhhhh...we just rinse it out, no problem and Big Ben don't have ta know every little thing , ya know?

Beth does the puppy trims, Bianca takes care of their nails, trim and paint, Betty keeps the books----Yeah, all

'B's .... last names' Bertinelli.....yeah, just like the movie star....You're a 'B' too.......Blister?......Oh, sorry! Bister! Yeah, easy mistake......brown?.. Really! Well, there's lots of browns...russet, sienna, chestnut, Moreno, marrone.... Yeah, you heard right, Moreno is a sort of dark brown, too.

Listen, ya wanna change your mind? Wouldn't take a minute to fix ya with a rinse to make those grays go away........yes, you do! Yes you do! Not many, but.....you do!

Well, OK....So pick a color for your nails....."

So, Samantha and Bernard walked back to Number Sixteen with new 'dos', one with bright red ribbons in his ears, a sparkle in his eyes and both with fire-engine red nails. Which turned out to be quite prophetic.

CHAPTER SEVENTEEN

Inbreeding causes 3 out of every 10 Dalmatian dogs to suffer from hearing disability.

Mamluk Tarik's chest swelled with pride--------finally, his new name!!!! A new person-----a new name! One that would resonate around the world..........all would quake with fear..... The uncertainty of his past....over. His new life just beginning. He felt himself on a precipice of great happenings. The fervor of his recent conversion was a bright, hot flame within him. He was astounded at the confidence he felt in his soul---his revelation was so near---what would it's form be? A voice? A vision? A flash of light......... bringing understanding?

Nervously, he struck matches, holding them until they burned his fingers, flinging them away over and over, the smell of sulfur, the heat, the tiny little bit of Hell, a small puff of light, the smoke as he blew it out or shook it until it went away in a smoky death, on and on, over and over, on and on......

.FLAME ! FIRE !! Of course! There it was! IT! The GREAT UNDERSTANDING!!!!

God is truly great!!!! er...er...Allah is truly great!!! That's the way now...Allah! Mamluk was on the way to the great things that would make his new name one of fear and admiration throughout the world!!!!! This was his calling!

Gosh! That didn't take long! He must be destined for something pretty terrifying and awesome since his gift, his enlightenment had come so soon....some of the followers had traveled to worship and study at the dusty feet of the turbaned in the motherland. He was so fortunate and so obviously called especially, because to fly in an airplane so far was not something he felt he could do.... Or even to travel across the seas......he knew no fear.....but he had seen the movie about the iceberg........

But, Tarik had been shown the way, had been enlightened without visiting foreign soil........he had a mighty gift! He was too smart to be talked into the ultimate, the suicide belt. Just the idea of wearing a bomb...which could blow up......the noise........well, no.

The gift of fire.......felt so right....so immediate......... how to begin......

****

Thus far, the mean streets had been at most, chilly. Sam and Bernie had ventured bravely to an unsavory section of the city, had gone into a crowded bar and grill, where Bernie had been treated to a hot ham and cheese ("Aw, c'mon, he's hungry") and a cold Miller Lite. They had walked past darkened department stores, now after business hours. They had talked to a patrolling city policeman who had stopped to talk with a youngish woman in very short shorts and very high-heeled shoes, who called Bernie 'Sweetie'. Fred followed discretely in his own car, a green Honda with an excess of 200,000 miles with the video camera, hoping for a crime, a riot, something worth while, something 'night beaty'.

And, Fred daydreamed about retirement.

As the night lengthened the three decided to just ride around for a bit longer, look here and there, and then, just call it a night---better luck next time.

Fred's police scanner, which had been mostly silent, muttering intermittently, erupted loudly, the dispatcher asking for back-up for crowd-control at a fire in the alley behind the Lucky Lindy Lotto and Liquor downtown.

They could see the ominous glow as the Honda gasped for a tiny spurt of speed. A dumpster wholly involved with flames, very near the delivery exit was being attacked by several firemen, the truck nearby. Smoke and steam swirled around the chaotic scene. Fred filmed the action as Sam and Bernie worked the crowd, interviewing onlookers and passersby.

The firefighters quickly gained the upper hand and the owner of the store brought out cold beer to them in appreciation. A party atmosphere soon ensued as the audience and the TV crew stood around and re-fought the conflagration, caught up on gossip, met Sam and welcomed Bernie.

Bernie enjoyed the attention and was lapping up his second brew when someone shouted, "Lookit! Another one!"

Firefighters and onlookers gasped to see more flames, more smoke as the next dumpster erupted. Bernie, left in mid-lap and raced down the dark alleyway, gripping a small struggling figure in what appeared to be pajamas with an odd headgear of some sort. Turban?

Bernie held the terrified squirming child firmly in his jaws until a policeman intervened.

"Malkie? Whaddya doin', Malcolm? Does your mother know you're out this late? Whaddya doin', Malkie? Tarik? What the hell's a tarik?....

New name? What the hell for, Malkie? Al what? Al who? Mamluk Tarik? Tarik Mamluk? Al kyda? Henry? Do you remember how to 'waterboard'?' We can use the fire hose---------- I think we got us a terrorist! Oh, fer cryin' out loud! Your Momma gonna be so proud of you ! She gonna come down on you..........Henry, call his Mother.....yeah, again....... I think he's just about to find out about the mother of all hot butts."

The owner of the Lucky Lindy Lotto and Liquor store brought out yet another case of refreshments and various war zones were discussed and political situations were analyzed and solved.

Samantha and Bernard finished the report with Fred's help, and everybody cleared out. Back at the station, in the late night, Fred and Sam edited the tape, while Bernie snoozed on the floor. This would make an interesting lead for the early morning show, 'Wide Awake in Wayne'.

When they returned to the big house, Sam and the hero warmed up the pasta pazzooo, or what ever Lola had called the dish of fabulousness, and celebrated.

And, did NOT go to that last room.

But, they walked past the door.......and thought.....

CHAPTER EIGHTEEN

It has been established that people who own pets live longer, have less stress, and have fewer heart attacks.

"............Yeah, I can hear you......Oh, you guys......aren't you nice........yeah, this is sort pf a big one...yeah,........... yeah ....yeah, the Big Five Oh.....yeah......well, thanks!

Yeah, I got it at the station........yeah, well, thanks for sending it on to me......yeah, it's a big deal to have such a rare type, I guess. Delbert, my boss saw it and wants me to go down to the blood drive and donate and do a report. About only one half of a percent of the population has this type and how we should donate......yeah, you know how I feel about that.....still creeps me out. But, since this is a new job and they did ask especially for me and Bernie......I guess I better grow up and just do it.

"Oh, he is the best thing! You know how I feel about Bernie!! He makes friends wherever he goes....You should have seen him at the beauty shop!!!! Yeah, it's for both... yeah, me too........

The gal who runs it,' Barbie'----she was talking about hair dye....I do NOT have grey hair.......I DO NOT!!! any way....she said one of 'em was named 'Moreno'.......I never knew that that was brown, too.......that murdered couple in Seattle.......wasn't his name 'Brown? Yeah, I know.....the blood types.....yeah, I know...don't match up.......I was just wondering.......yeah, I couldn't be...........It just seems odd, that's all........with 'bister' being brown, ...yeah, I know, there are lots of words that mean 'brown' and it's just weird.......Oh, yeah, that guy, John Brown was running from something and whatever it was, came out and got him.... yeah, oh, well........just odd...

Yeah, we're settling in.....I think we're living in a crime scene......there's one room Bernie won't let me go in and that's the one that has the new carpet and the fresh paint. Yeah, I think so too...And it seems like almost every body is 'connected' one way or the other. But you know, they are all so nice to me and Bernie. Yeah, I think it may work out.

Well, a few......no, not brown recluse.....not hobo spider, either.......well, I might have accidentally......

well, I won't, any more. No really....I won't... Yeah, I know, they are our friends.....I am not mocking you !......

You betcha!!!!! Thanks for thinking of me.....yeah I will....Yeah I will........Yeah, I can hear you......Oh, you guys! How sweet! Awhhhhh! No, none of you can sing.........Thanks, you're making me homesick......and many more..........Yeah, I heard him....yeah, he sounded awful..........Well, thanks.....Yeah well,.....yeah......well...... OK ....bye."

Sam clicked the phone to 'off' and sighed. Bernie, sharing the couch laid his great head in her lap and sighed too.

"Yeah, Bernie----Happy Birthday to me.........every year people dress up and have fun on my birthday...... happy, happy birthday--------------------------"

CHAPTER NINETEEN

The wolf's massive rear molars aid in cracking and crushing bones.

The high-school counselor, faced with the realities of drug and alcohol abuse among the students, texting or talking on cellphones, speeding, sometimes simultaneously and the general mayhem teens are prone toward, believing themselves immortal, loaded a bunch of the little darlings up on a bus and took them to the tri-county morgue in Newark. Delbert, hearing of this, sensed blockbuster TV and assigned his new protégées to the story.

"Listen, this'll be great television! You'll do fine! Oh, yes, it'll be creepy, for sure! Our ratings will be dyn--o--mite!"

Samantha thought to herself, "Hoo--boy!" Fred Moffett, looking forward to a cozy retirement in just one more year and eleven months, loaded the video camera and thought about desert islands and sunshine.

Bernie thought about going for another ride with his beloved Samantha.

The counselor fervently hoped to shock this latest herd of young people out of the chemically/hormonally induced fog they perpetually moved about beneath.

Thinking only of their clothes, face, hair, body, last night, the week-end and how unfair life was, how awful old people are, the target group slouched sullenly from the bus and into the vestibule at the foreboding block building.

This being a planned event, three uniformed policemen, the coroner, and two of his assistants handed out latex gloves, stained green protective gowns, blue bonnets and clear shields to protect them from being splashed with bodily fluids.

Samantha and Bernie and Fred plus shoulder cam had arrived early and were filming set-up shots and interviewing as the group assembled.

"Alright, people, can I say a few words here...excuse me, can I have your attention?......Hello!!! HELLO?! .... OK, as you know this is the morgue and I am the medical examiner, or coroner. Our business is to determine how death occurred...naturally or if a crime has been committed. We do not pre-suppose anything. I hope I don't have to tell you not to touch any of the bodies."

An uncomfortable chuckle went through the assemblage as the door opened. For hinges to creak would have been too much of a cliché, but appropriate. White-shrouded body-size bundles lined the walls, piled several high. Disinfectant was the dominate odor, not unpleasant but persistent. Fluorescent lights hummed in the brightly lit room........otherwise, quiet reigned........and something.... was .....different.

Bernie checked out the living. Though strictly speaking, official regulations forbade canines to witness anything in the M E's domain, but, (and it was a large but) everybody wanted to be on TV.

The living numbered enough to be a small crowd and with the dead...claustrophobia threatened.

"If you feel uncomfortable, leave the room. There's is nothing to be ashamed of if you feel ill, just do not make a mess in here. We all experience death in unique ways. For some of you, this will be your very first time.
What you are about to observe is death that has come by several different methods: violence, drugs, car crash, accidents of many kinds........and nature. Please be respectful. Remember, this is how we all end up."

Mr. Clark had made this very speech in the classroom but without the same impact.

Samantha and Bernie, trailing Fred, moved among the youngsters in their professional capacity, interviewing... observing, the dog quietly hovering close to his beloved, a comforting presence, a calming influence.

"As you can see, we are in the process of autopsying this young man who was discovered unresponsive at his home, by his mother. We have here a young man, 20-28 years of age, 180 pounds, no obvious signs of trauma. He had a history of alcohol abuse but had been attending rehab.

So, we are ready to make the classic 'Y' incision, beginning at each shoulder, joining at the breastbone and continuing down the center past the navel."

A few of the young people crowded closer to get a good look. Others held back, and one or two moved to touch something for support of some kind. A kind of tearing sound emanated throughout the sterile area.

" As you can see, this exposes the ribcage which we will need to open to get to the heart and lungs. We use ordinary bolt cutters to break the ribs.............."

Starting as a low, humming...growing to a quavering moan, louder now softer now a moan, now a cry, now a visceral wrenching sob.....

"What the???!!"........... One of the patrolmen, hand on his pistol searched the room....

Bernie, in full cry now, threw back his massive head and gave vent to the blood cry from his heritage of ancient pre-history.

Behind the shields and above the masks and under the bonnets, the students' eyes enlarged and blood drained from their faces.

The M.E. Glanced around at his audience, and satisfied that he had engaged their attention, continued the task.

CRR-R—RR-ACK.........CR-A-CK.

"And here we have the lungs---,"

He lifted the tissue from the chest cavity and began slicing with an ordinary butcher knife.

"Let's do a section---------some tar----------beginning deterioration... we find that even light smoking damages the lungs and other organs immediately.... see what happens when you smoke?------and the heart........well, look at that!"

He placed the dripping heart on a scale but returned to the gaping hole in what was once a perfectly healthy young man.

"An awful lot of blood in the pericardium.....the sack around the heart.------ OK-----OK------here's the culprit right here! This aorta otherwise looks healthy, except for this tear here, which leaked a large amount of blood into the pericardium and stopped it. This is probably the cause of death, but, let's move on to the liver ......Alcohol use shows up here, as you can see by the color of the organ and the hardening on the edges....? As we open the abdomen and stomach, we discover that this young man had had as his last meal what looks to be a hot dog, with relish and mustard, can you smell it? This other stuff is just some undigested matter, maybe some sort of salad.......... He probably would have had something a little better had he known this was gonna be the last meal.

I think we have found our cause of death, but if we are going to do an autopsy, let's do a complete one. Harvey, bring the saw."

While the attendant readied the special vibrating saw, the coroner made a single incision on the vertex of the skull and pulled the scalp forward, exposing the bone. The high, whining sound of the vibrating saw slicing through bone permeated the room.

The assistant handed the M.E. A small key-like utensil which was inserted into the aperture in the white bone and the skull-cap popped off with a slight sucking sound.

"We can remove the brain and section it to see if any sign of trauma is evident or lesions of disease are visible. We will weigh it and take tissue samples like we did from the other organs"

Every one in this small, intense place felt small and very much mortal.

"I believe this young man had a history of cocaine use. His mother was not aware of this and had hoped he could be rehabilitated from the alcohol problem. So, I'm just supposing on this one, but, we will not make judgment until after toxicology gets back to us"

The attendants took samples, weighed organs, replaced everything back into the body cavity, sewed the scalp back over the naked skull, hiding the incision on the back of the head, sewed the body back up using the baseball stitch, hosed the blood off the gurney onto the concrete floor and down the drains.

"The responsibility now is passed on to the undertakers. Questions? "

The students were much more subdued, now, but very interested and asked about what they had witnessed.

"So, his mom didn't know he was on coke?"

"How long did he smoke?"

"How old was he?"

"How long can you keep a body before it starts to stink?"

"Do you have bad dreams?"

"Have you ever had a body wake up while you were cutting on it?"

"Do you cut up girls the same way?"

"Do any of the bodies ever fart?"

The counselor stepped in: "O.K., O.K.,...... I believe that's enough.....Thank you, gentlemen and ladies for your time and patience. I think the students have learned a great deal here and maybe it will make a difference in how they go about their daily lives. Thank you, again."

As the coroner de-gloved and removed his mask and splash shield he looked at the big, black, sad dog.

"I can say unequivocally, that we have never had an accompaniment at one of our 'openings' before."

"Bernie has deep feelings sometimes....sorry. We will probably keep that piece of tape in our story, though. Everybody likes to see Bernie on the news."

"You betcha!!!! When will it be on?....................Be a really good one for Halloween.........! Dead bodies creep a lot of folks out.....I don't see it, myself.....It's the living ones that you have to watch out for........"

CHAPTER TWENTY

The wolf's front teeth are sharp and pointed and adapted to puncturing, slashing and clinging.

Her birthday!!! Fifty years.......where does the time go?..........odd, how life runs along....

Maybe some have a plan, a blueprint, mileposts to reach, accomplishments to achieve..........

For so long, it seemed, Samantha had been moving toward.............something. This would be another new experience, one she dreaded. Other people donated blood and lived, how bad could it be....what could happen?

Red Cross banners festooned the sidewalk and parking lot of the massive stone church. Samantha and the cameraman, led by Bernard entered the vestibule where they were met by an unfortunate personage who had evidently been in a terrible accident of some sort that had forced her head into a very odd angle.

"So glad you have decided to feature us on your newscast. We need the publicity and more donations.... Take lots of pictures, just ask permission first, some folks are camera shy, for one reason or another.

Well, hi, Bernard! What a handsome creature you are! No, don't worry; he'll be just as welcome as anybody else.

We wondered if you would mind.........you'd be perfect! Hate to spring this on you but you look like a good sport.....we had planned....

Would you like to be Little Red Riding Hood? And Bernie could be the Wolf? You could stroll around and do your reporter thing.....It would be perfect.....Oh, would you?"

She proffered an elaborate hooded cloak in such a brilliant hue of red that Samantha instinctively recoiled.

Sam had always avoided red, sometimes nearly gagging at certain tones of the color. She couldn't logically understand her reactions, phobias being mostly unexplainable to most.

But, today was a milestone birthday. She was in a brand new job, new place making new friends, and her best friend was close by her side.......Plus, this looked like it could be fun.....

"Of course! We would be honored! And I have never donated before.....I keep getting these cards, and......"

"Just step on inside......they'll take good care of you and you can get all done up after your donation...No problem. And thank you so much...Oh, my head?.....looks pretty gross doesn't it? My story is that I was kept in a jar from baby-hood on so that my parents, who were gypsies could rent me out to traveling circuses.........Pretty good, I thought, but it takes a long time to get in costume. But you know? Halloween only comes once a year..... celebrate!"

An attractive girl with alarming fang marks on her throat and a stethoscope dangling nearby met her inside the door.

"Your first time to give? Well, we need some info first thing.. Nothing much.... Been abroad lately? .... Yeah, I know....there's a joke there....but.......

Oh! Look at you! You're special!!! The Big Bloodsucker sent you an invitation!!!! AB negative, even! Congratulations! Just follow the 'Bride' and she'll get the paperwork started."

Snickering at her own joke she continued: "Her 'hubby,' Big Frank looks mean, but he falls to pieces at the sight of blood..............really.....I should stop....but this is really funny stuff......."

The fellowship area of the church, 'St. Brigit of the Fields' had been transformed into a Halloween-themed donation facility for the Red Cross. Several donors either sat or lay chatting or reading as life leaked into plastic bags suspended from the gurneys.

Medical personnel who had gotten themselves up as various bloody personages circulated, attending to the tasks and trying not to have too much fun at the expense of the more woozy of the attendees. Dracula s and the ax murdered predominated, with a few car accident victims mixed in for variety, checking the bloody harvest.

As donors finished, they moved to the cafeteria side of the large room where volunteers of some church or organization served juice or coffee and sandwiches or cookies or chips.

One lone volunteer sat knitting at a card table covered with cards and pins to reward those who had given, over time, gallons and gallons of life. She appeared to have been strangled lately, the pantyhose still tight around her neck.

Black and orange clashed merrily with the red and white crosses and over the sickly sweet stench of freshly bagged blood, hilarity ensued.

Samantha allowed herself to be questioned and having evidently passed the exam, her arm was tourniquet ed, painlessly needled (she looked away) and type AB negative flowed away.

She thought of Halloweens past, anything but needles and blood and red, struggling with this new adventure. This was a silly thing, really, to be so frightened of a color....

Bernard had sized up the unlikely scenario before him, sniffed food, glorious food among all the other odors in the large room, the freshly drawn blood and the bleeders and chose, surprise! Food. The servers, after a brief flurry of near hysterics: "Is that a bear? It looks like a bear! How's a bear get in here? The Allerghetti's had a bear in their back yard last week! Is that a bear? Well, it sure looks like a bear!" were charmed and Bernie chowed down.

Samantha, surprisingly still alive after the traumatic donating process which proved to NOT be traumatic, donned her disguise and had her juice and cookie with Bernie and his new buds. Refreshed they began their duties, visiting, gathering information from fellow donors, trailed by Fred and his video-cam (he had donated also, O negative), and making good television.

A disturbance across the room drew their attention.

A tiny elderly woman accompanied by an attentive, very attractive fellow, probably her son was protesting at some length.

"Listen, I've been giving blood here since before you were born! I know the ropes! I am AB!! Negative !! I have answered all those dam' questions a million times!!! I have an invitation...!

Where's my nurse? I always come and give on my Nicci's birthday!!!!! Have I ever told you about my Nicci? She was stolen from me! That dam' Renae Amortuzzio and Gianni Moreno stole my Nicci!"

"Now, Ma, these nice people have heard all about Nicci....See? Here's your nurse, er, vampire....every thing will go just fine, now......Then we'll go out to the cemetery just like always, right, Ma?"

"Just a half pint this time, Mrs. Buongiovanni. We are so grateful for your dedication over the years. AB negative is an extremely rare blood type, as you well know. You have saved a lot of lives. Thank you!"

"I do it for my Nicci, every year, I do it for her....did I ever tell you how she was stolen from me?! That dam' Renae took my Nicci...."

"A tragedy! All done, Mrs. Buongiovanni! Come, let me help you to you juice and sandwich----- Tony, so nice to see you...I know your mother appreciates your thoughtfulness in being with her for this..... Hey, Little Red Riding Hood here is a first time giver.....and she's an AB negative, too...."

The nurse, who had suffered a nearly fatal wound to her neck, escaped the familiar tirade from Mrs. Buongiovanni.

"Here you go, Ma. Orange juice and chocolate cookies.... .Little Red Riding Hood? And the Wolf? Well, you look good.....We been watching you on the tube. You look familiar, you from around here? Your name is...?

"Nah, I don't want to be on t.v.....Point that thing some other way....."

Fred felt a chill from Tony's steady gaze and immediately moved to film on the other side of the room.

" I been seeing your dog and you on the tube.............. Samantha Blister? What kinda name is that ? It ain't Italian, is it? Well, you sure look familiar......"

"It's BISTER, not Blister.....someone told me the other day that it means a shade of brown."

" AB negative, eh? You and Ma, same type, go figure..."

"Did I hear you say your name was 'Buongiovanni'? Are you in business around here? Do you ever go over to Wayne? I live on Eton Court........"

Then it was Samantha's turn to feel a coolness around Tony. His eyes appraised her steadily, thoughtfully.....

Samantha scooted along the bench, making room for the older woman and her attentive son. Ever the reporter she said," I couldn't help overhearing, your baby was kidnapped? Did I hear you say one of the kidnappers was named 'Moreno'? Someone told me the other day that that was another word for the color brown....my name, Bister, does, too.........."

Tony continued his appraisal......Eton Court....... thorny bushes.............

Others at the table suddenly finished and left.

His mother said, "Today is my Nicci's 50th birthday! I always give blood on Halloween for my baby.......That dam' Renae Amortuzzio and Gianni Moreno stole her from me............."

And Sat Down Beside Her.